THOMAS CRANE PUBLIC LIBRARY
QUINCY MASS
CITY APPROPRIATION

PARACHUTE REGIMENT

SPECIAL FORCES: PROTECTING, BUILDING, TEACHING, AND FIGHTING

AIR FORCE

ARMY RANGERS

ELITE FORCES SELECTION

ESCAPE AND EVASION

GREEN BERETS

MARINES

NAVY SEALS

URBAN WARFARE

PARACHUTE REGIMENT

WORLD'S BEST SOLDIERS

PARACHUTE REGIMENT

by Jack Montana

Mason Crest Publishers

Copyright © 2011 by Mason Crest Publishers. All rights reserved. No part of this publication may be reproduced or transmitted in any form or by any means, electronic or mechanical, including photocopying, recording, taping, or any information storage and retrieval system, without permission from the publisher.

MASON CREST PUBLISHERS INC.
370 Reed Road
Broomall, Pennsylvania 19008
(866)MCP-BOOK (toll free)
www.masoncrest.com

First Printing
9 8 7 6 5 4 3 2 1

Library of Congress Cataloging-in-Publication Data
Montana, Jack.
  Parachute regiment / Jack Montana.
       p. cm.— (Special forces : protecting, building, teaching and fighting)
  Includes bibliographical references and index.
  ISBN 978-1-4222-1845-7
  ISBN (series) 978-1-4222-1836-5
   1. United States.—Armed Forces–Parachute troops–Juvenile literature. 2. United States.—Armed Forces.—Airborne troops.—Juvenile literature. 3. Parachuting.—Juvenile literature. I. Title.
  UD483.M66 2011
  356'.1660973.—dc22
                                         2010025185

Produced by Harding House Publishing Service, Inc.
www.hardinghousepages.com
Interior design by MK Bassett-Harvey.
Cover design by Torque Advertising + Design.
Printed in USA by Bang Printing.

With thanks and appreciation to the U.S. Military for the use of information, text, and images.

Contents

Introduction   6
1. History of Parachute Use in the Military   9
2. Paratrooper Training, Safety, and Techniques   17
3. Air Force Pararescue   29
4. Army Parachute Teams   43
5. Navy Parachute Teams   53
6. Paratroopers in the Marines   65
7. Paratrooper Missions Around the World   79
Find Out More on the Internet   90
Further Reading   91
Bibliography   92
Index   94
Picture Credits   95
About the Author and Consultant   96

Introduction

Elite forces are the tip of Freedom's spear. These small, special units are universally the first to engage, whether on reconnaissance missions into denied territory for larger conventional forces or in direct action, surgical operations, preemptive strikes, retaliatory action, and hostage rescues. They lead the way in today's war on terrorism, the war on drugs, the war on transnational unrest, and in humanitarian operations as well as nation building. When large-scale warfare erupts, they offer theater commanders a wide variety of unique, unconventional options.

Most such units are regionally oriented, acclimated to the culture and conversant in the languages of the areas where they operate. Since they deploy to those areas regularly, often for combined training exercises with indigenous forces, these elite units also serve as peacetime "global scouts," and "diplomacy multipliers," beacons of hope for the democratic aspirations of oppressed peoples all over the globe.

Elite forces are truly "quiet professionals": their actions speak louder than words. They are self-motivated, self-confidant, versatile, seasoned, mature individuals who rely on teamwork more than daring-do. Unfortunately, theirs is dangerous work. Since the 1980 attempt to rescue hostages from the U.S. embassy in Tehran, American special operations forces have suffered casualties in real-world operations at close to fifteen times the rate of U.S. conventional forces. By the very nature of the challenges that face special operations forces, training for these elite units has proven even more hazardous.

Thus it's with special pride that I join you in saluting the brave men who volunteer to serve in and support these magnificent units and who face such difficult challenges ahead.

—*Colonel John T. Carney, Jr., USAF–Ret.*
President, Special Operations Warrior Foundation

CHAPTER 1
History of Parachute Use in the Military

The first known image of a person using a parachute dates from the 1470s. Shortly afterward, in 1485, Leonardo da Vinci developed a parachute. These early designs for parachutes were different than those we currently use. They were pyramid shaped and functioned differently than what we know as the parachute. They were also made of heavier materials than we currently use. The first parachutes makers stretched linen over a wooden frame to create their parachutes.

> "Where is the prince who can afford so to cover his country with troops for its defense, so that ten thousand men descending from the clouds might not, in many places, do an infinite deal of mischief before a force could be brought together to repel them?"
> —Benjamin Franklin, 1784

The modern parachute was invented by Louis-Sebastien Lenormand to jump out of hot-air balloons. After first landing a dog, Lenormand jumped out of the balloon successfully in 1783. Blanchard made the breakthrough between the concept of the parachute in Renaissance times and the modern parachute: he replaced linen and wood with folded silk, which is a much lighter material. He also took out the clumsy wood frame, which was needed to sustain the parachute in Renaissance times but was no longer required with the new materials. It was not until later, when airplane combat in World War I began, that parachutes were used as a safety device in planes.

WORLD WAR I: A NEW WAY OF FIGHTING BEGINS

World War I started the use of a number of technologies that defined twentieth-century war technology. Machine guns, land mines, and airplanes were used for the first time on a massive scale to inflict damage against enemies. With these technologies, trench warfare began, where armies dug large, long tunnels in the ground to combat enemies. And World War I was the first time in which parachutes were used in combat situations.

Armies used observation balloons that flew high above the trenches to report the enemies' activity. Usually, observation balloons held two soldiers, equipped with parachutes.

History of Parachute Use in the Military

This was the intended purpose of the parachute when it was modernized by Lenormand: to safely land from a balloon.

The Allied forces (which included America and Britain) did not provide parachutes for pilots in airplanes. The British thought that having parachutes on the aircraft would encourage cowardice. For most of the war, the technology to make safe parachutes had not been developed anyway. Not having a parachute no doubt did provide motivation for the Allied pilots: if they needed to get out of the aircraft and it was an emergency, they could either jump out of the plane (without a parachute!) or land the plane safely. Toward the end of World War I, the German air force was the first to issue a parachute to all pilots.

During World War I, planes were much more primitive than they are now. Many of the air battles that took place were called "dog fights"—fights literally between two individual airplanes, as shown in this World War I re-creation. If one of the planes went down, the pilot had no choice but go down with it.

PARACHUTES IN THE WAR-ZONE

Following the end of World War I, the U. S. Army began testing parachute troops in combat zones. At a demonstration in San Antonio, Texas, six soldiers were able to parachute

> ### Da Vinci Parachute
> In 2008, Swiss adventurer Olivier Vietti-Teppa tested Leonardo da Vinci's drawings. He used the pyramid-shaped parachute to safely drop 2,000 feet. However, he did not use the original materials that da Vinci used; Vietti-Teppa's parachute had no wooden frame, and the material of the parachute was also updated.
>
> French parachutist Adrian Nicholas used the design and the same materials. Nicholas did not drop the whole way by only using da Vinci's parachute, however; at 2,000 feet from the ground, he used a modern parachute to reach the ground.

from a bomber, land, and have their weapons ready for action within three minutes. At the time, military planners were not convinced that parachuting troops into a battle zone was the best approach.

Then, during World War II, Germans successfully parachuted troops during their invasion of Europe. The Germans were so effective that U.S. branches of the military began to develop their own specialized teams and incorporate airborne **deployment** into branches of the U.S. military.

History of Parachute Use in the Military

PARA-CHUTE
The word "Para-" comes from the Italian word meaning "to guard against, counter." "Chute" is the French word for "fall." The word parachute literally means "to stop people from falling too quickly."

The first airborne infantry unit to see combat was deployed in Algeria (North Africa) in November 1942. The paratroopers were also a part of the invasion of Normandy, one of the most crucial moments in the entire war. Paratrooper units have been used ever since: from performing special missions in Vietnam to parachuting into Afghanistan today.

In August 1943, twenty-one troops crashed their airplane into an uncharted jungle in Burma near the Chinese border. The only way for a medic to help the injured men until they could get to safety was to drop down from a plane. Lieutenant Colonel Don Fleckinger and two medics brought the injured troops back to health enough to leave the jungle safely. After this, the military saw the need for a force that could airdrop into a location where there is a fallen soldier and quickly give them medical help; the idea for the PJs—the Parajumpers—had been born.

UNDERSTAND THE FULL MEANING
deployment: The process of putting military personnel into place for action.

14 PARACHUTE REGIMENT

World War II paratroopers on D-Day, leaping from the sky to do battle against Germany.

The U.S. Military started the Air Rescue Service (ARS) in May 29, 1946. While the ARS is not limited to paratroopers, they are a vital part of its mission. The PJs have served their country in every major war since then.

"We're Not Heroes"

They say that aren't, but they are. The 101st Airborne 501st Parachute division landed behind enemies in June 1944 during the invasion of Normandy, one of the central turning points in World War II. When they entered enemy territory, many missed their landing position, and more than a thousand were killed or captured. Once they were on the ground, they had difficulty finding each other and giving their coordinates for reinforcements. After they had, though, they pressed onward, taking over the town of Carentan and holding it down, even in the face of a Nazi counter-attack.

Some of them fought all the way to one of Hitler's retreats, called the Eagle's Nest. The Eagle's Nest was built for Hitler's fiftieth birthday; workers had decorated it lavishly. Hitler's Nest even included an elevator that went straight down inside the mountain where the Nest was built.

Although these soldiers were partially responsible for the Allied invasion's victory, at a recent reunion of these now elderly paratroopers, they were humble about their place in history. "We're just regular people.... We just did what we were supposed to do," one of them stated. But paratroopers changed the course of history.

CHAPTER 2
Paratrooper Training, Safety, and Techniques

Paratroopers can serve in the Army, the Navy, or the Marines—but they all begin their training as paratroopers at the U.S. Army Airborne School located in Fort Benning, Georgia. For three weeks, they are trained by the "Black Hats" of the 1-507th Parachute Infantry Regiment.

AIRBORNE SCHOOL

During Ground Week, soldiers practice landings and in-aircraft procedures. The second week, Tower Week, soldiers practice exiting an aircraft out of mock towers and landing off the swing lander trainer. The third week is Jump Week, where soldiers must complete five successful airborne operations. Typically, the first two jumps are conducted wearing

18 PARACHUTE REGIMENT

only the parachute, reserve chute and harness (referred to as "Hollywood" jumps), followed by two jumps wearing full combat gear and finally, a night jump. After the successful completion of five jumps out of a high-performance aircraft, soldiers are awarded basic parachutist wings. This badge allows the now paratrooper to be assigned to an airborne position within an airborne unit.

During paratrooper training, students begin by jumping from buildings, rather than airplanes.

Paratrooper Training, Safety, and Techniques

Once assigned to an airborne unit (one with designated Paid Parachutist Positions (PPP)), paratroopers will continue to train during airborne operations and can participate in combat jumps if required. Officers are eligible for additional training in an Advanced Airborne School offered at Fort Bragg, by the Eighty-Second Airborne Division, and at Fort Benning, by the 1-507th, upon the successful completion of twelve paratroop jumps. Tested areas during the jumpmaster course are Nomenclature, Sustained Airborne training, pre-jump oral recitation, a written exam, Practical Work in the Aircraft (PWAC), and the Jumpmaster Pre-Jump Inspection (JMPI). After the successful completion of Advanced Airborne School, paratrooper graduates are then referred to as "jumpmasters."

Senior Parachutist Wings are paratroopers who are jumpmaster qualified but have not yet met the requirements for Master Parachutist Wings. Master Parachutist Wings are held by the most seasoned of jumpmasters.

BASIC PARATROOPER SAFETY

American paratroopers receive training in a number of areas to ensure they arrive in the battlefield safely. They are taught how to respond to their parachute opening too early in the aircraft. They learn how to push their static line into the hands of the safety or jumpmaster to prevent the line from getting tangled around the next jumper, and the proper procedures in case the aircraft has an emergency.

Most important, they learn a system of steps. If paratroopers perform these steps while jumping, they should successfully reach the ground from the aircraft.

Before each airborne operation, a jumpmaster runs through the "Sustained Airborne Training" script. While the script is recited, paratroopers perform the actions they will do when jumping from the aircraft. The jumpmaster watches them to make sure each step is done correctly. When you're about to fall hundreds of feet through the air, safety is important!

STEP ONE

The first point of performance is: "Proper exit, check body position, and count." Here, the eyes are open, the chin is on the chest, elbows are tight into the sides, and the hands are over the ends of the reserve parachute with fingers spread. The body is bent slightly forward at the waist, with the feet and knees together and knees locked to the rear. This position ensures that the jumper does not tumble on leaving the aircraft; it also means the parachute will open correctly. On exiting the aircraft, the paratrooper slowly counts to four (one thousand . . . two thousand . . .); if no opening shock is felt, the reserve parachute is immediately activated.

STEP TWO

The second point of performance is: "Check canopy and immediately gain canopy control." To gain canopy control of the MC1-1D parachute, the jumper reaches up, secures both toggles, and pulls them down to eye level, simultaneously

Adjudant Loic Neveu, an instructor at the French Parachute School, steps off the tailgate of a U.S. Air Force C-130 Hercules cargo plane during a combined airborne operation with American paratroopers in Pau, France.

making a 360-degree check of his or her canopy. To gain canopy control of the T-10D parachute, the jumper reaches up, secures all four risers, and simultaneously makes a 360-degree check of his canopy.

STEP THREE

Once control of the parachute is gained, the third point of performance is: "Keep a sharp lookout for all jumpers during your entire descent." This includes the three rules of the air:

- Always look before you **slip**.
- Slip in the opposite direction to avoid collisions.
- The lower jumper has the right of way.

A fifty-foot separation must be maintained between all jumpers all the way to the ground.

STEP FOUR

The fourth point of performance is: "Slip into the wind and prepare to land." At approximately 200 feet (60 m) above ground level, a check is performed below the jumper and then the equipment is lowered. When jumping with an MC-1D parachute, the turn into the wind is performed approximately 200 feet (60 m) above ground level. If the wind is blowing from right to left, the right toggle is pulled and the

UNDERSTAND THE FULL MEANING

slip: Turn away.

Paratrooper Training, Safety, and Techniques

elbow locked. Once facing into the wind, the toggle is let up slowly to prevent twisting. If the wind is blowing from the jumper's rear to his front, either toggle can be pulled. If the wind is blowing from the jumper's front to her rear, only minor corrections need be made to remain facing into the wind. When jumping a T-10D parachute, the slip into the wind is performed at approximately 100 feet (30 m) above ground level. If the wind is blowing from left to right, the jumper reaches up high on the left risers and pulls them down into his chest, holding them until landing. If the wind

Teams get securely fastened to their parachutes prior to conducting a spot jump. Teams were scored depending how close they landed to the designated marks.

is blowing from the rear to her front, she will reach up high on the rear risers and pull them down into her chest and hold them until she lands. If the wind is blowing from the jumper's front to his rear, the front risers are pulled down into the chest and held until landing. After the jumper has slipped or turned into the wind, she assumes a prepare-to-land position by keeping the feet and knees together, knees slightly bent, elbows tight into the sides, chin on the chest, and eyes open.

STEP FIVE

The fifth point of performance is: "Land." A parachute-landing fall is made by hitting all five points of contact: balls of the feet, calf, thigh, buttocks, and the pull-up muscles. One of the canopy release devices is activated while remaining on the ground to prevent being dragged across the ground by the parachute. The harness can then be removed—and the paratrooper is ready for his mission!

PARACHUTING TECHNIQUES

Airborne forces use many different techniques when parachuting inside borders. Secrecy is important; the element of surprise is one of the most effective tools against the enemy.

> "To command a parachute unit, you don't have to be nuts, but it helps!"
> —Colonel Howard R. Johnson, first commander of the 501st Infantry Regiment

Paratrooper Training, Safety, and Techniques 25

Sergeant First Class Geronimo Blancaflor, a rigger instructor with the Quartermaster School's Aerial Delivery and Field Services Department, inspects the new T-11 parachute worn by Sergeant First Class Timothy Vogt.

HALO PARACHUTING

Most **elite** soldiers know how to perform a static line drop, which means that a large number of troops jump from an aircraft and parachute down. This method is usually too slow, and transport aircrafts can easily be shot down. So the military designed new methods of parachuting.

A New Parachute for Today's Soldiers

In 2009, military planners and engineers helped create the T-11 parachute, a new design that reduced the landing impact by about 49 percent, a feature that will be beneficial to the health of troops. The T-10 was useful, but today's troops carry more equipment, and the equipment they carry is heavier. The lighter T-11 will make combat safer—and be much easier on the legs of soldiers.

A swifter, more secret way is called High-Altitude, Low-Opening (HALO) parachuting. Troops jump from an aircraft at an altitude of 32,000 feet (10,000 m). They do not open their parachutes immediately, but instead, freefall until 2,500 feet (760 m) and then open their parachutes. This means they get from the aircraft to the ground quickly and are less likely to be found by the enemy.

HALO parachuting requires a large amount of training. The free faller has to keep a stable position during the flight while wearing a heavy backpack and weapon strapped to his body. At high altitudes, the HALO jumpers need oxygen-breathing equipment. The fall is so fast that HALO parachuting requires a machine called a "**barometric** trigger" to automatically open parachutes at the right altitude. The difficulties don't stop there: paratroopers are exposed to freezing temperatures as they freefall. This can result in ice forming on their equipment, especially their goggles. HALO jumpers need to be in prime shape and highly skilled. The U.S. military spends a large amount of time training for HALO jumps. Only the best elite units train their soldiers in HALO techniques.

HAHO PARACHUTING

Other techniques are also used to transport soldiers safely behind enemy borders. HAHO parachuting stands for High-Altitude, High-Opening. Paratroopers drop from an aircraft wearing oxygen-breathing equipment at an altitude of 32,000 feet (10,000 m). They freefall for only 8 to 10 seconds and then open the parachute around 27,600 feet (8,500 m). They then slowly and silently float to the ground. This can take between 70 to 80 minutes, and they travel for up to 19 miles (30 km). This means that the team can drop outside enemy territory and drift behind enemy lines unseen by radar.

There are problems with HAHO parachuting. The Special Forces team must stay together once parachutes are opened to land in the same location. Winds can scatter people for miles, so this is difficult. Soldiers must be experts at using parachutes to land close together.

UNDERSTAND THE FULL MEANING

elite: Superior in quality.

barometric: Having to do with measuring the pressure of the atmosphere.

CHAPTER 3
Air Force Pararescue

"To protect the United States via air and space": this is the fundamental goal of the U.S. Air Force, and it is why soldiers join the Force—to protect their country, its people, and its interests. Within the branch, though, there are several smaller and more specialized branches, known as Special Forces. Each of these is more physical, more extreme, and just as honorable and important a job as any in the military. Pararescue is one of these special **tactics** teams. Becoming a member of the pararescue troops requires as much, if not more, specialized physical and intellectual training than a job in the general Air Force would.

UNDERSTAND THE FULL MEANING
tactics: Detailed military maneuvers to achieve specific goals.

Pararescuemen in the U.S. Air Force are unique in several ways. First, they are the only **Department of Defense** special force that is specifically trained and equipped to conduct any kind of rescue operation—**conventional** or **unconventional**. They are the first troops called upon for a search-and-rescue mission and **personnel** recovery, and they are among the most highly trained specialists in the United States Military. Their motto, "That Others May Live," is what pararescuemen, or PJs (short for parajumpers) as they are commonly known, work to achieve. They are committed to self-sacrifice and saving others, both fellow servicemen and civilians.

DUTIES

Pararescue forces enter combat zones to come to the aid of wounded troops. They are highly specialized forces: trained in combat, the use of parachutes, and the ability to provide medical help during stressful situations.

UNDERSTAND THE FULL MEANING

Department of Defense: The U.S. department in charge of all military action.

conventional: Done in the standard way.

unconventional: Referring to warfare that involves unusual methods, such as surprise attacks behind enemy lines, sabotage, and working to persuade locals to join them.

personnel: Individuals in an organization.

Pararescuemen jump from a HC-130P/N for a High-Altitude Low-Opening (HALO) free-fall drop from 12,999 feet in support of Operation Enduring Freedom.

REQUIREMENTS AND SELECTION

There is a Special Operations unit of the U.S. Air Force in charge of rescue missions performed by troops jumping out of airplanes and using parachutes. Pararescue is a difficult branch of the Air Force to join; you need dedication and a genuine interest in helping other troops.

The official websites states that to join the Pararescuemen, you must be able to:

- Swim 25 meters underwater on one breath.
- Swim 1,000 meters using the sidestroke or freestyle in 26 minutes or less.
- Run 1.5 miles in under 10 minutes and 30 seconds.
- Pull off eight chin-ups a minute or less.
- Do 50 sit-ups in two minutes or less.
- Complete 50 flutter kicks in two minutes or less.

The website also suggests that there are other ways to stand out from other applicants:

- Run three miles in under 21 minutes.
- Do 50 to 60 correct push-ups in two minutes.
- Do 100 to 130 sit-ups over a four-minute period.
- Do 12 pulls or chin-ups correctly.
- Swim 1,500 meters in less than 28 minutes.

If accepted, there is a training period to go through that lasts for almost a year. All recruits receive training to

Air Force Pararescue 33

Pararescuemen must be as skilled in the water as they are in the air. Here, soldiers fall toward the water, with their flippers already on their feet so that they are ready for a watery landing.

34 PARACHUTE REGIMENT

A PJ's primary function is as a personnel recovery specialist, with emergency medical capabilities in humanitarian and combat environments. PJs deploy in any available manner, to include air-land-sea tactics. PJs participate in search and rescue, combat search and rescue, recovery support for NASA and conduct other operations as appropriate.

become fully qualified emergency medicine technicians. They also learn advanced land navigation, light weapons usage, escape techniques, and survival techniques. Not only do they learn combat skills but also skills that pertain to medicine. Paratroopers learn chemical warfare survival and various medical rescue techniques appropriate for warfare situations.

GETTING HIRED

The Air Force is currently evaluating how to get more cadets and keep them. A large number of applicants are not qualified to be in the PJs, and the ones that are have difficulty completing training. On average, 15 to 20 percent of trainees graduate to be pararescue members. As an example, in 2007, 69 of 480 cadets finished PJ training.

When a candidate shows great potential, many military branches compete to hire them. If you show that you are highly qualified and are strong willed, the Air Force may give you generous offers to join the PJs. Even if you test high and are in great shape, however, training will be challenging.

TRAINING

PJs undergo some of the toughest training in the entire military. They must complete the same training as any EMT-paramedics, plus additional physical and specialized training.

36 PARACHUTE REGIMENT

U.S. Airman First Class Kevin Freyre drags Airman First Class Nathan Greene to safety at a simulated helicopter crash scene during a mass casualty incident exercise at Kirtland Air Force Base, New Mexico. The exercise is part of the pararescue recovery specialist course at the Pararescue and Combat Rescue Officer School.

INDOCTRINATION COURSE

This orientation takes place on the Lackland Air Force Base in Texas. It is a ten-week course that teaches PJs medical terminology, weapons qualifications, PJ history, physiological training, and extensive physical training.

U.S. ARMY AIRBORNE SCHOOL

All PJs attend the Airborne School in Fort Benning, Georgia (discussed in chapter two), where they learn basic parachuting skills and static line airdrop in a three-week course.

COMBAT DIVER COURSE

In Panama City, Florida, at the U.S. Air Force base, PJs learn to use SCUBA and closed-circuit diving equipment to become combat divers. They are trained for over six weeks, and learn to **covertly** take over areas, conduct sub-surface searches, and perform basic recovery operations.

UNDERWATER EGRESS TRAINING

At the Naval Air Station in Pensacola, Florida, trainees are taught specific skills over just one day of instruction, learning how to safely escape from a water-crashed or sinking aircraft.

BASIC SURVIVAL SCHOOL

PJs spend two and a half weeks at the U.S. Air Force Base in Fairchild, Washington, learning basic survival techniques for remote areas. Training includes principles, procedures,

---

UNDERSTAND THE FULL MEANING

covertly: Secretly.

MOTHER'S DAY

In May 2010, Jody Gomez had a difficult Mother's Day. Her eighteen-year-old son Zachary Warner was joining the Air Force the following week. His goal was to join the elite pararescue program. His mother was apprehensive, but she knew her son always went for difficult goals. She, like so many other military mothers, wonders, "How is it possible to be so proud and so heartbroken at the same time?"

equipment, techniques to survive in extreme climates and harsh environments, and how to return home safely.

FREE-FALL PARACHUTIST SCHOOL

This five-week course in Fort Bragg, North Carolina, and the Yuma Proving Grounds in Arizona teach **wind tunneling**, and in-air instruction on things such as aerial maneuvers, air sense, and parachute opening procedures.

PARAMEDIC COURSE

The longest course in a PJ's training, this EMT-paramedic certification lasts twenty-four weeks at Kirtland Air Force Base in New Mexico. Trainees learn field medical care and

UNDERSTAND THE FULL MEANING

wind tunneling: Going into a structure resembling a tunnel, where air is blown at known velocities for training purposes.

Air Force Pararescue 39

A young Hurricane Katrina survivor hugs her rescuer, Staff Sergeant Mike Maroney, after she was rescued and relocated from her home. Maroney is a pararescueman from the 58th Rescue Squadron.

PARACHUTE REGIMENT

Jumpmaster

"Jumpmaster" is a respected military title used for a specialist in airborne deployment and combat. Jumpmasters supervise other paratroopers jumping off a plane. To train, you must go through a nearly month-long process. Not everyone makes it. For instance, when training in October 2009, 37 out of 51 trainees became jumpmasters when training in Fort Carson, Colorado. The title of jumpmaster is looked at highly because of the great responsibility that comes with holding the position. In Colorado, the training officer Patrick Clark states the importance of being a jumpmaster: "This a job that we take seriously because every jumpmaster is responsible for every parachutist and the number-one rule is never sacrifice safety for any reason." Attention to detail is especially important because "a lack of attention to detail can result in lost lives. From the time the jumpmaster receives the order until the time everyone is on the ground, the jumpmaster is responsible."

extrication basics, field tactics, mountaineering, combat tactics, advanced parachuting, and helicopter insertion/extraction. They become qualified as pararescue recovery specialists for assignment to any pararescue unit worldwide.

UNDERSTAND THE FULL MEANING

extrication: The process of getting something or someone out of the current surroundings.

MISSIONS AROUND THE WORLD

Pararescue teams are used in America's twenty-first-century conflicts, saving the lives of their fellow servicemen whenever they are in harm's way. They also assist foreign countries

> ### Profile: Why Join Pararescue Forces?
> When Ben Priddy, a twenty-one-year old from Elizabethtown, Kentucky, was interviewed by a local newspaper, the *News Enterprise*, he talked about why he chose to join a Special Forces unit for the Air Force. Ben stated in jest, "It was pretty much that or Burger King for me." Eighty-five percent of applicants are not able to complete pararescue training, but Ben looked forward to the challenge and the "adrenaline kick." Ben also stated that he was attracted to the fact that the military program focused on saving life instead of ending it.

in need of help. For instance, in January 2010, the United States Special Forces helped the Haitian government rescue victims of an earthquake. Combined with international teams, they rescued a total of 134 people affected by one of the largest recorded earthquakes.

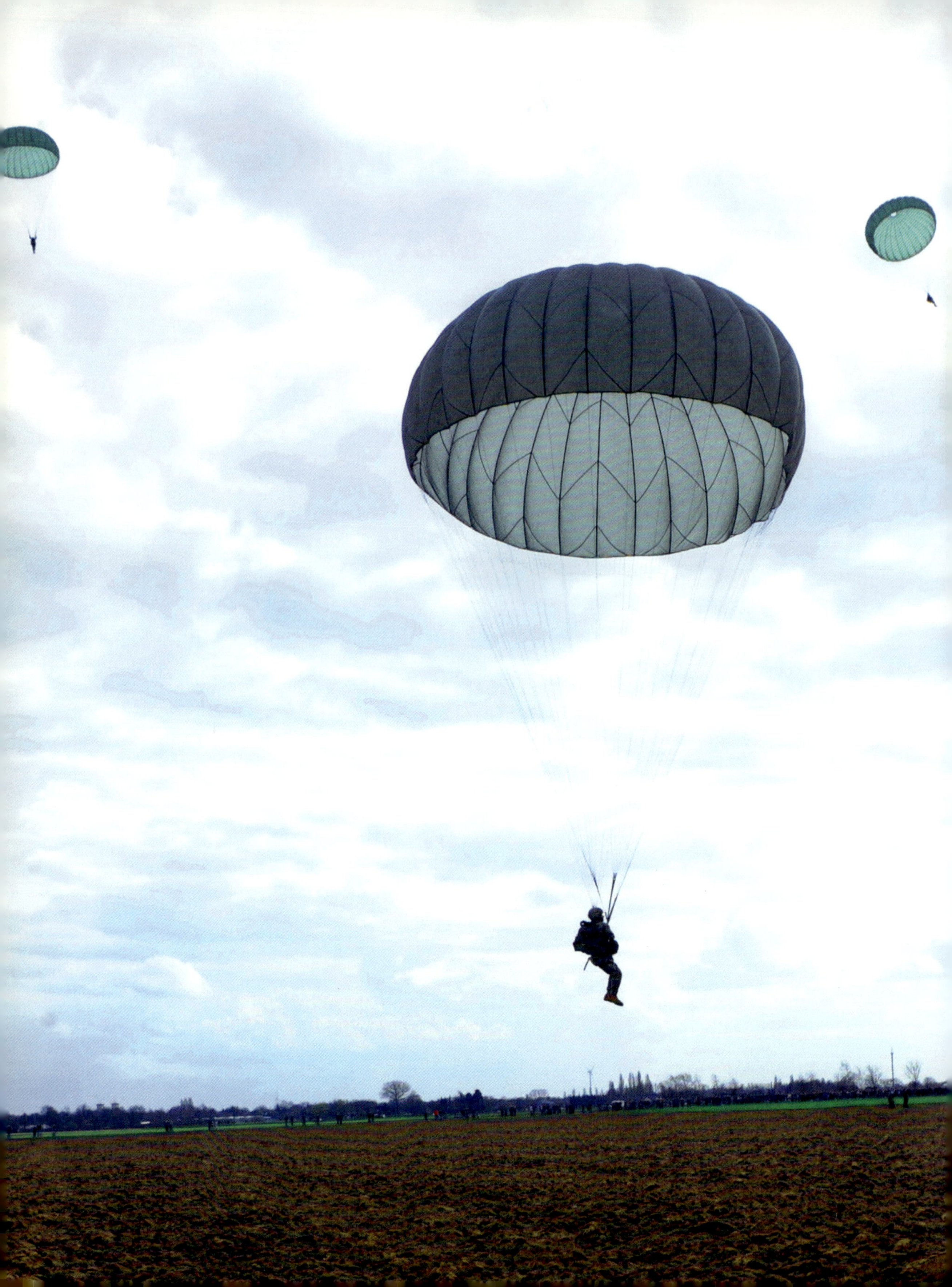

CHAPTER 4
Army Parachute Teams

Airborne army units are valuable to the U.S. military because of their ability to deploy quickly into a combat zone. If used correctly, paratroopers provide an element of surprise. For instance, in World War II, specialized teams would parachute inside enemy lines to confuse Nazi troops while conventional soldiers attacked on the ground. The enemy was more vulnerable and weaker to fight because of the effectiveness of American paratroopers.

Currently, paratroopers are used across the country for a variety of missions. Air-assault teams drop down from helicopters and directly engage enemy forces. Parachute teams are especially effective in blurring battle lines, confusing the enemy while they relentlessly attack them. They do not only see direct battle but sometimes also become involved in missions that aid the military. They may parachute into hostile

Taliban-occupied wilderness to perform **reconnaissance** missions, or they may be used to provide relief for victims of natural disasters.

When the United States needs paratroopers to perform special missions, they are ready to serve their country.

HISTORY OF THE AMERICAN EAGLES

When Major General William C. Lee activated the 101st Airborne Division he told recruits who not yet seen combat that they had "a rendezvous with destiny." Lee went on to say, "We shall be called upon to carry out operations of far-reaching military importance."

Since the Airborne Division began, airborne troops performed missions across the world, surprising the enemy at every step. Their badge is the great American eagle, a bird that crushes "its enemies by falling upon them like a thunderbolt from the skies." This is why the parachute regiment proved so effective during World War II: quick airborne deployment stunned Nazi and Japanese troops.

When air-assault teams were first deployed in World War II, they were used in both the Pacific **theater** of war and the European theater. In Europe, they were deployed in Holland, Normandy, and Italy. On the Pacific front, air troopers landed before conventional troops.

UNDERSTAND THE FULL MEANING

reconnaissance: The process of looking around behind enemy lines to find out useful information.

theater: A region in which active military operations are in progress.

Troops of the 82nd Airborne Division jump en masse, during a demonstration at Oujda, French Morocco, North Africa, on June 3 1943, shortly before the Sicily invasion

TRAINING IRAQI TROOPS

It is a mark of the progress that the Iraqi army has made that U.S. Army paratroopers can now train Iraqi forces in airborne deployment. Sergeant Bryan Caldwell, who has conducted airborne operations with other countries, stated he felt confident parachuting with the Iraqis. "I think we'll come together . . . when it's time and see something amazing."

From their beginnings in World War II, Army airborne troops proved themselves tenfold. Since World War II, the American Eagles have fought in all major military conflicts, from Vietnam to the first Gulf War. After September 11, 2001, they answered the call of duty once more.

DUTIES

Army paratroopers have all of the duties of a foot soldier. They must be able to be **self-sufficient** during missions, be able to use firearms, and be in good shape. They also need to be leaders and show an aggressive spirit. Paratroopers need to know the basics of being a soldier, but they also must be more than proficient at parachuting. They need to be experts in combat and in airborne deployment. One skill is not more important than another; a soldier who shows

UNDERSTAND THE FULL MEANING
self-sufficient: Able to manage without outside help.

Bad Jumps

It was an unexpected worst-case scenario for Matthew Hutcheson. He was ready to parachute out in a training mission in Fort Bragg. Nothing in particular seemed wrong that day; no one thought he would run into an issue. While they flew into the sky in the small aircraft, all involved were confident. Hutcheson's unit had reviewed procedures for air deployment problems. He had forty-seven jumps under his belt and was ready for a successful number forty-eight.

As he jumped out, he start to count the seconds—and then he realized he was stuck to the plane. The equipment he was using was hooked to something; the airplane was towing him. As soon as the plane crew knew that he was being towed, they communicated with Hutcheson to make sure he was conscious. When they realized that he was, they performed Army protocol without hesitation. They flew the plane to a higher elevation and cut his cord, and then Hutcheson used his backup parachute. His foot became tangled in the reserve parachute but he untangled it before the parachute was fully open. Remarkably, he had not a single injury afterward, even though there had been several opportunities for disaster.

Army leaders involved in the training stated that Hutcheson's experience with air jumps was a key part of why he was able to save the situation. Sergeant Poindexter, who oversaw the operation, said that Hutcheson's actions were "textbook. . . . It reinforced everything we've practiced. The training works. The way that we practice it, the way that we rehearse it—when it comes down to it, you just follow what you've been taught. It works."

> ## "GERONIMO!"
> The United States Army organized the first parachute combat unit, the 501st Parachute Battalion. While performing a jump early in their career, a soldier began a longstanding parachuting tradition. Private Aubrey Eberhart yelled out "Geronimo!" to prove to a friend that he was in full control of his faculties while he was jumping. He did not know that he had just invented a tradition among airborne warriors. The saying caught on among the 501st Division and is still used by paratroopers today.

excellence in parachuting but is a weak soldier will not be effective in attacking the enemy. On the other hand, a fierce warrior who shows a lack of safety when using parachutes will not be an effective paratrooper. Paratroopers have two sets of skills and need to show excellence in both. The standards to be a paratrooper are set very high; anyone who is interested in joining airborne defense groups must know they can maintain those standards.

REQUIREMENTS AND SELECTION

An applicant to the Army paratroopers must:

- Be younger than thirty-six when they apply.
- Physically qualify for parachute duty.

Army Parachute Teams 49

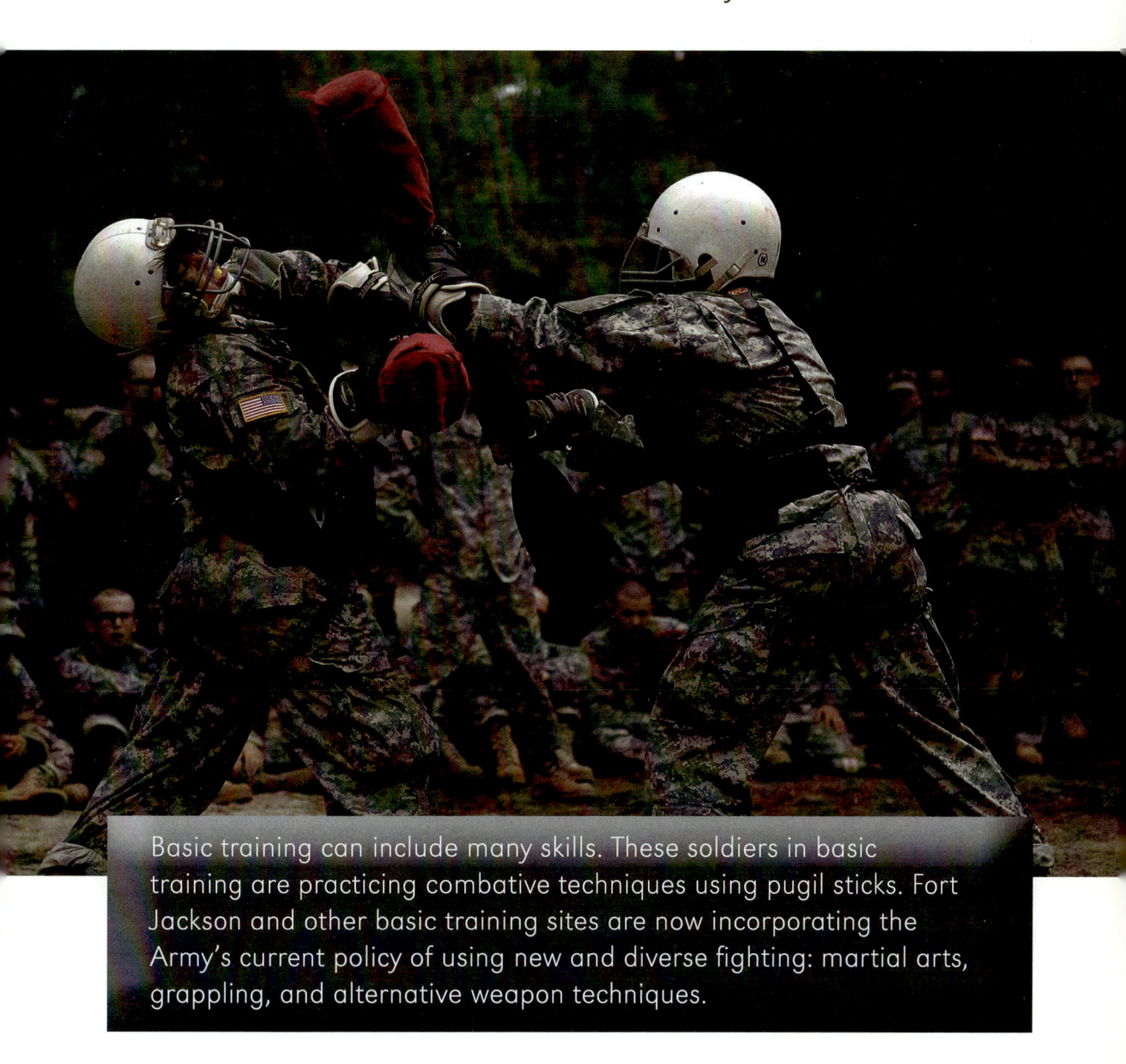

Basic training can include many skills. These soldiers in basic training are practicing combative techniques using pugil sticks. Fort Jackson and other basic training sites are now incorporating the Army's current policy of using new and diverse fighting: martial arts, grappling, and alternative weapon techniques.

- Pass the Army Physical Fitness Test (APFT) with a score of 180 points or more.
- Have already completed Basic Training.

Good Times / Bad Times: Keeping a Sense of Humor

Sergeant Simon Baum of the Parachute Infantry Regiment just won't let it go. He's still upset about his iPod. He jokes that his reason for returning to combat is to avenge the iPod, broken from a bomb blast that left him severely wounded. He was listening to Led Zeppelin when his truck hit the bomb. "I heard 'Bad Times' and that's the last thing I remember."

His first memory after the blast is all blood and shrapnel, broken glass and craters. A medic dragged Baum out. His wrist and leg were severely broken. He suffered from torn cartilage and many small cuts. Later, doctors diagnosed Baum with mild traumatic brain injury. But he never lost a sense of humor; even while he was only semi-conscious, he made his brothers-in-arms laugh.

Doctors have found in scientific studies that humor can provide mental health benefits for the effects of stress, pain, and conflict. It makes burdens seem lighter, hopeless situations seem more hopeful and confusing situations seem more controllable. By laughing, we acknowledge the fact that we may not be able to control the situation, but we also make the statement that we will make the best of what's given. Laughter fits the military mindset perfectly.

Now that Baum is rehabilitated and back in his combat unit, he says, "I understand the real danger of what I'm doing," but he's still excited about being able to return to combat. Just two days before being re-deployed in Afghanistan, his wife discovered she was pregnant with triplets. "I still don't think I've let that sink in," he said.

Now if only he could get over that iPod. . . .

Army Parachute Teams 51

Sergeant Simon Baum, an infantry team leader with the 508th Parachute Infantry Regiment, 82nd Airborne Division, was wounded in an IED attack in 2007. He found out his wife was pregnant with triplets two days before returning to Afghanistan.

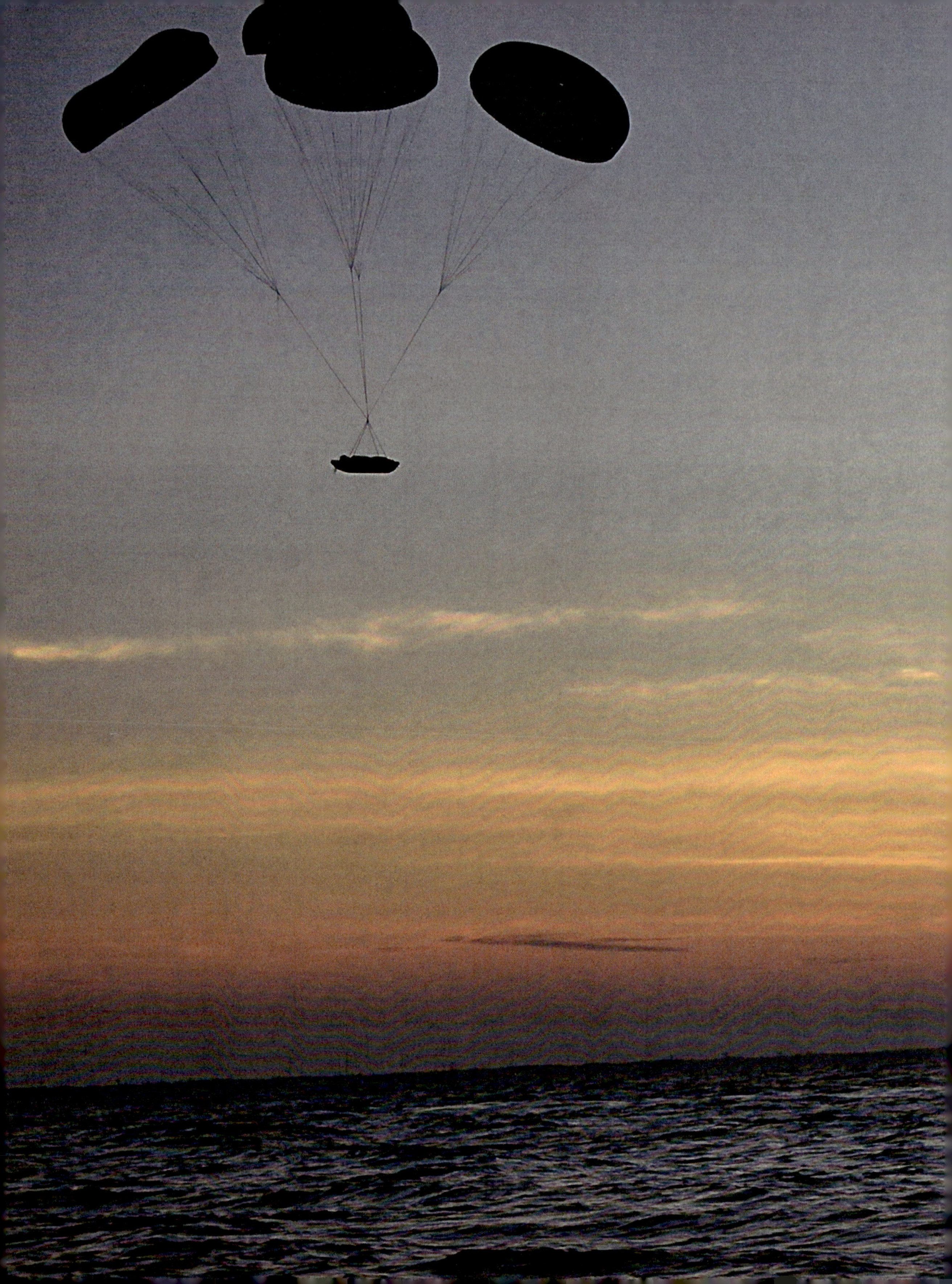

CHAPTER 5
Navy Parachute Teams

When we think of the United States Navy, we usually only imagine a force of ships operating for the U.S. military. However, in combat, the Navy uses the air as well as the sea. The U.S. Navy has more airpower than any other military power in the world, second only to the United States Air Force. The Russian Air Force is reported to have 2,749 airplanes in their arsenal; the United States Navy has 3,700.

The Navy wages war by air through specialized teams that make full use of parachute technology. The SEALs are the main Special Operations unit for the Navy.

They can deploy by parachute at any time (SEAL stands for Sea, Air, Land). The Navy also uses parachute technology for special units besides the SEALs, including bomb disposal teams and Maritime Special Operations Forces.

> "Ready to Lead, Ready to Follow, Never Quit"
> —*Official Navy SEAL Motto*

HISTORY OF THE NAVY SEALS

President John F. Kennedy (a World War II Navy veteran) foresaw the need for a trained force to fight unconventional warfare in future overseas conflicts. He increased funding for Special Operations units, and Areligh Burke, Chief of Naval Operations, recommended **guerrilla** and anti-guerrilla units. He wanted those units to be able to operate on sea, land, or air. The military began basic SEAL **indoctrination**-training classes. Soldiers learned to fight hand-to-hand combat; they also learned to perform high-altitude parachuting and set up demolition devices; and they studied foreign languages. The first SEAL teams were commissioned in 1962.

Since the beginning, the Navy SEALs achieved excellence in all that they did. Deployment by parachute is important to many of their missions. The element of secrecy and immediacy of specialized forces landing in an area has always been an effective tool for the SEALs.

In 1983, President Ronald Reagan ordered the invasion of Grenada, calling upon the Navy Seals to rescue Paul Scoon, a politician under house arrest. Nine SEAL forces

UNDERSTAND THE FULL MEANING

guerrilla: A kind of warfare that uses surprise attacks and sabotage behind enemy lines.

indoctrination: The process of teaching someone to accept a set of ideas.

Students assigned to a Basic Underwater Demolition/SEAL class participate in Rock Portage at Coronado Island. Rock Portage is one of many physically demanding skills that are a part of First Phase training.

were deployed by parachute to rescue the governor. One of two transport planes missed their drop zone, and four SEALs drowned in violently bad weather.

Once they entered, they had forgotten important communications equipment to request backup. They were sur-

> ### Attitude Counts!
> When going through training, the NAVY SEALs lose from 70 to 80 percent of their applicants. Ten percent of students don't have the physical ability to make it through training. Another group of people, around 10 to 15 percent of them, will make it through training so long as they are not injured. What is the difference between those who make it and those who don't?
> Motivation.
> While all the applicants are considered fit enough to train for Special Forces, you cannot teach attitude as easily as physical fitness. If you enter training with the attitude of a warrior who can overcome any obstacle, you have a higher chance of succeeding.

rounded by Grenadian and Cuban troops. Using a telephone in the mansion itself, the SEALs called in for backup. They were pinned down in the mansion overnight. Marines came in for backup and rescued the troops along with the governor.

While it was a successful mission, it is a reminder that invading a country by parachute is filled with risk!

Navy Parachute Teams 57

U.S. Navy SEALs and German forces freefall parachute onto a frozen lake in Northern Norway during Exercise Cold Response 2010.

A SEAL student moves through the weaver during an obstacle course in the first phase of training at Naval Amphibious Base Coronado. The course is one of many physically strenuous exercises that are part of the seven weeks of first phase.

REQUIREMENTS TO JOIN THE NAVY SEAL TEAM

An applicant for the NAVY SEALs must:

- Be a man.
- Be younger than twenty-nine.
- Have excellent eye sight, without any color-blindness issues.
- Score at the required standards for the Armed Services Vocational Aptitude Battery (ASVAB).
- Be a U.S. citizen.
- Pass a physical examination for divers.

To be eligible, a rigorous physical test is required. To pass the physical test, you must:

- Swim for 500 yards within 12 minutes and 30 seconds.
- Complete 42 push-ups in 2 minutes.
- Complete 50 sit-ups in 2 minutes.
- Complete 6 pull-ups. There is no time limit.
- Run 1.5 miles by at least 11 minutes and 30 seconds.
- Pass an underwater demolition physical test.
- Complete boot camp training.

SEAL TRAINING

Once an applicant has been chosen for the SEALs, the real training begins. The first phase of SEAL training lasts eight weeks. In the first phase, the soldiers learn to be comfortable in the water, work as a team, and make their bodies fit. The physical tasks—which include running, swimming, and calisthenics—become harder as time goes on. Recruits take weekly four-mile timed runs; they must get through timed obstacle courses; and they swim long distances. The fourth week of phase one, called "hell week," is the hardest. The military tries to see if a candidate for the SEALs will crack under pressure. To do this, they simulate what a high-stress mission is like.

In the second phase of training, SEAL candidates condition themselves to be combat swimmers. Trainers focus on

Training

Navy SEAL Thomas J. Valentine had served his country in both Iraq and Afghanistan. Though he had seen combat, and received many medals for courage under fire, he tragically lost his life during a parachute training operation.

Lieutenant David Luckett stated, "This is a stark reminder that what these warriors do on a daily basis is very dangerous, both on and off of the battlefield."

Training often involves simulating what occurs during combat. Be sure during training to be as alert as you would be in combat.

scuba diving skills. While the trainees learn techniques for diving, they continue extensive physical exercise.

The third phase lasts nine months. This phase trains candidates in the use of weapons and explosives. After the

Students navigate their way through the chaos of smoke and explosions in one of the final activities of Hell Week. On average, students are allowed only two hours of sleep during Hell Week, and those who complete it have about a 95 percent chance of graduating.

Crewman Qualification Training SEALs candidates check the rounds assembled before a night weapons training with lasers on a remote range at Camp Pendleton. CQT is a fourteen-week advanced training course that teaches basic weapons, seamanship, first aid, and small unit tactics.

> **COST OF TRAINING A SEAL**
> The Navy SEALs are selective about whom they train, because the process is expensive and time-consuming. Training a single Navy SEAL can cost up to $500,000. Training a single person comes with risk; the military makes sure it makes a good investment when they choose their recruits.

instruction on combat, trainers continue to make physical tasks harder for their students. The running distances become longer, and the passing times are lower. In the final three and a half weeks of training, the trainee applies all the techniques they learned.

The SEALs can be used anywhere the United States needs a special operation. Some units specialize in working in a specific continent or area in the world, but Navy SEALs are prepared at any time that military intervention is needed. Within the past few years, the SEALs have assisted the Navy and Army in our two most recent wars, Afghanistan and Iraq. They have also aided the United States in specialized missions.

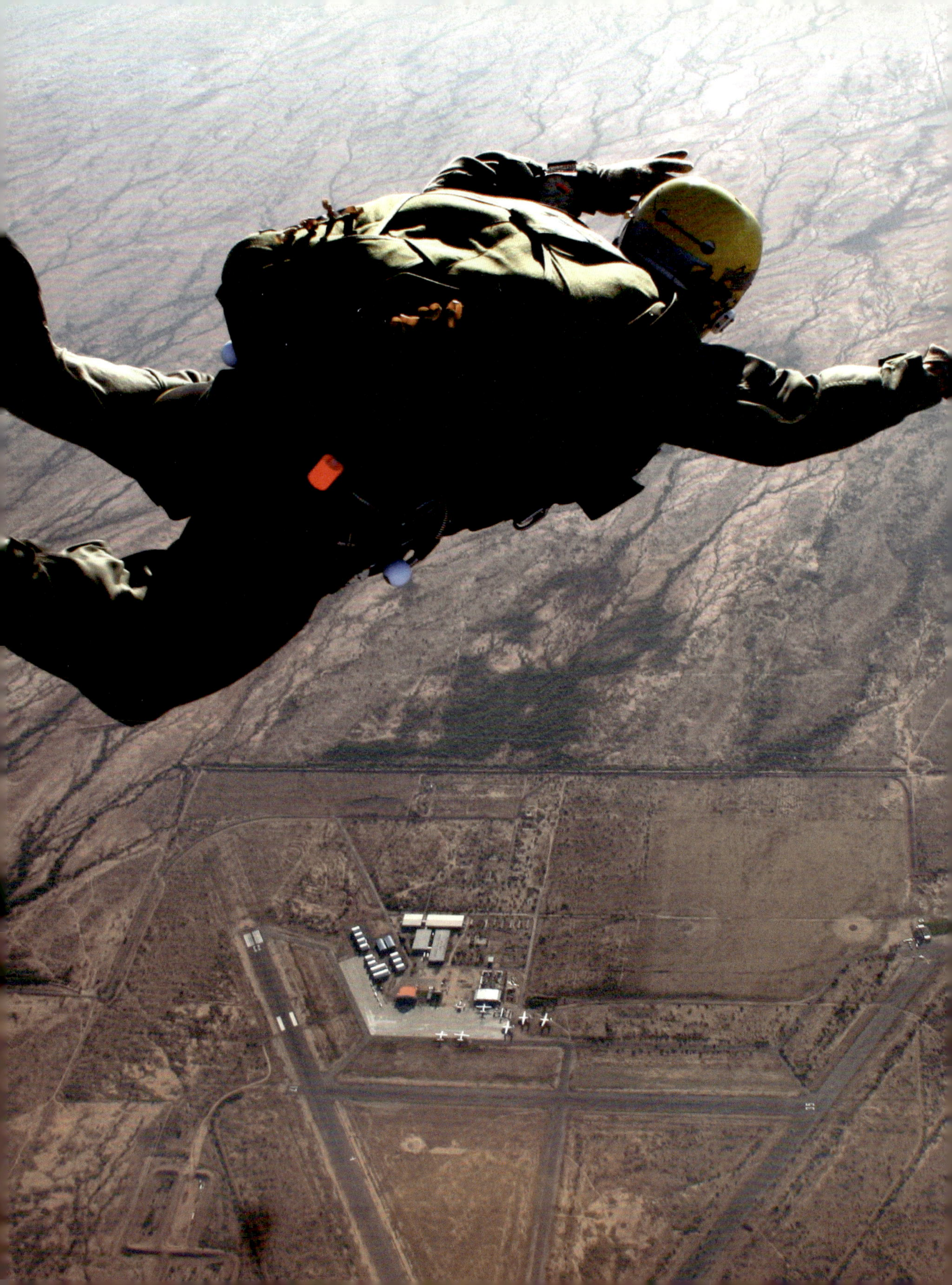

CHAPTER 6
Paratroopers in the Marines

The Marines are used for reconnaissance missions as well as combat. Reconnaissance, which literally means "to recognize" in French, involves collecting information from a military enemy. Usually troops infiltrate enemy lines to confirm an enemy's presence and the state of their military. Reconnaissance is not just the collection of information for the sake of information; rather, it is used to prepare the troops for a potential attack.

There is a subtle difference between spying and reconnaissance. Spying (also known as espionage) involves information gathering by government officials who do not see combat and may not always be used for military purposes, while reconnaissance is information gathering for military units, by military units.

The United States Marine Air-Ground **task force** uses many different ways to collect information on an enemy. One means at their disposal is to parachute down into enemy territory. The Marines enter enemy space through high and low altitudes. By using parachute technology, they are able to infiltrate into enemy territory without the enemy knowing they are there.

As Sun Tzu states in the ancient book, *The Art of War*, "If you know the enemy and know yourself, you need not fear the result of a hundred battles." The Marines' reconnaissance teams are crucial to the military's ability to collect information on others. The parachute has become one of the major tools in reconnaissance.

HISTORY

Early in the twentieth century, Major Dion Williams conceived of the Marines using a variety of different methods to collect information. In 1906, parachute equipment was not as popular nor was submarine technology as useful, but all that would change as the century progressed.

After World War I, Major Williams expanded the way in which the Marines would incorporate new technologies into reconnaissance missions. Airplanes and submarines would now be used for observation. Long-term information gathering became valued as well.

UNDERSTAND THE FULL MEANING

task force: A temporary military unit put together to accomplish a specific purpose.

The Marines were useful in providing reconnaissance during World War II. Later, in the Korean War, the Marines performed their parachute insertions into enemy territory for reconnaissance missions.

DUTIES

The Marine Corps Special Operations unit performs specialized missions abroad. Their duty when doing reconnaissance

The Marines served their country well during World War II. Here, they are shown crossing a muddy jungle stream in the South Pacific.

U.S. Marine Corps parachutists free fall from an MV-22 Osprey at 10,000 feet above the drop zone.

work is not to be seen by the enemy and to collect as much information as possible. All information is used, not only information on numbers of troops but also information on the weather and general conditions in the enemy area.

REQUIREMENTS AND SELECTION

It takes more than combat skills and the ability to parachute to be a successful undercover Marine. Several other skills are needed as well. An elite soldier should be able to learn a new language and speak that language fluently, which means they can comfortable speak without stumbling over words or using awkward phrases. They should also have good relational skills; this means being able to negotiate with people. Undercover soldiers must have the ability to impersonate people if they want to blend with foreign peoples on an operation. By observing the way people dress, speak, act, and think, they are able to imitate these characteristics.

Undercover soldiers must be able to keep a secret. Those that want to go undercover to brag about it are never accepted for the job. The U.S. military trusts soldiers to keep highly secret information. If soldiers boasted about their work to parents, spouses, and friends, they would put lives in danger. In some cases, undercover soldiers must hold these secrets for the rest of their lives.

TRAINING

Not everyone is allowed to be a Marine. To join this elite unit, you have to show that you have the right character and intelligence to fight for the reputation of the Marine Corps.

The U.S. Marine is one of the most highly trained soldiers in the world. An average Marine must be courageous, intelligent, able to make decisions quickly, capable of leading men or women into action, good at communicating, writing, and mathematics, and also be able to handle all the weapons at his or her disposal. Because so much is required, trying to get into the Marines is incredibly difficult.

WHAT IT TAKES TO JOIN

Before they can become a Marine, recruits must convince their recruiters that they are suitable. Then they must survive the training program, one of the toughest in the world.

All Marine recruits have a long interview before they are allowed to begin training. First, recruits are tested for their level of physical toughness. But they are also assessed for their character and personality. Marine recruiters will probe deeply into the applicants' histories to find moments of courage, determination, or leadership, which may indicate what they will be like as a future Marine. If the individual has struggled through poverty to gain a good education or support a family, this might indicate strength of mind. If the person has a criminal record, he or she will be rejected immediately; Marines must respect society and people.

Gradually, the recruiter will come to understand the people being interviewed, and form a judgment as to whether they are suited to be a Marine. Though they may have strong characters, they must also display another mental quality demanded by the Marine: intelligence. All Marines take long intelligence tests. These test skills such as English and mathematics. All Marines must show above-average scores on the tests, making them one of the most intelligent military units in the world.

All soldiers must display intelligence, but those in elite units must have a higher than average intelligence. This makes the members of the Marine Corps excellent at working

A Marine student is dragged through a pool at the Aviation Survival Training Center to simulate an ejection seat being pulled by a parachute in water. The Training Center at Marine Corps Air Station Miramar, California, provides aviation physiology and water survival training for pilots and aircrew.

out problems and making decisions on the battlefield. Also, military psychologists have studied how intelligence affects the way people fight. They discovered that people who really threw themselves into battle were generally more intelligent than those who did not. They were also better at working out tactics that could win battles. In the elite units like the Marine Corps, an intelligent mind is a must.

The Marines also need people in control of their emotions. People who are violent, unpredictable, or unsociable will never make good Marines. To be a Marine, you have to be able to discipline yourself. This means doing dangerous, long, boring, or difficult jobs without complaining, and also doing them to the best of your ability. Elite units tend to work in small squads or even as individuals. All soldiers must be able to do their jobs because other people's lives depend on them. A soldier's own self-control could be the only thing that makes a mission a success. Elite forces also spend more time watching and waiting than fighting. They must also be able to deal with the crushing boredom of long, solitary watches while staying alert. Not everything is exciting as leaping out of an airplane with a parachute strapped to your back!

However, neither do the Marines want people who do not give enough effort. Elite forces' missions tend to require high levels of aggressive commitment. Marines have to have flexible minds that can work out a problem, but they also must pursue their missions with total dedication. This is the quality we call "mental endurance," and it is this that is tested during training.

Men assigned to an Explosive Ordnance Disposal (EOD) mobile unit collect their parachutes and move from their landing zone after a free fall jump from 10,000 feet in Bahrain.

Five Reasons Why People Fail Boot Camp

The following are a common list of misconceptions and bad attitudes about boot camp. Try to do the opposite of these things:

- Lack of preparation: You may think you have worked out enough because you went to the gym a few months prior to starting boot camp, but the physical fitness required to be a Marine does not come quickly.

- Lack of a personal drive: It is important to always remember why you joined the Marines. Write down the number-one reason you are joining the military and always look at it while you are in boot camp. This should guide you through difficult times.

- Lack of tenacity: A drill sergeant is not there to be pleasant. They are there to break down any attitudes or assumptions about the military. Their goal is to shock you into military life. They want to form you into a soldier so that you will be prepared when it is time to perform for your country.

- Lack of prior knowledge: You will have a rush of new information when you join boot camp. A "smart book" will be handed to you once you get to

For the Marine, there is no such thing as "basic" training. Entering the Marines requires that soldiers undergo incredible physical punishment. For twelve weeks, they will be shouted

basic training. The smart book includes: marching procedures, a phonetic alphabet, and other military traditions. Knowing these things ahead of time will give you an edge. Especially important may be: knowing the phonetic alphabet, knowing general orders, and understanding how to read military time. If Woody Allen was right when he said, "80 percent of success is showing up," then the other 20 percent is preparation. This leads us to the final reason why trainees fail boot camp.

- Lack of mental preparation: Not being in a good state of mind is the easiest way to fail boot camp, even easier than not being prepared physically. Being prepared in your mind ahead of time goes even farther than the other four reasons on this list. If you know that you have made the right decision and you never lose sight of that purpose, then the different obstacles appearing in your path won't seem so difficult to overcome. Once you are prepared in your mind, you are already partly there. Waking up at five in the morning, being screamed at, your face landing square into the mud-filled ground—these things seem less terrible when you are mentally prepared.

at, forced to run many miles with heavy packs on their backs, deprived of sleep for days at a time, and have to make decisions almost every waking minute. During that time, the candidates are watched to see what their characters are like. The drill instructors are looking for particular qualities.

COURAGE

Throughout their history, the Marines have fought in battles where the odds against them seemed overwhelming. What they need are men and women who will not crack under pressure even when things seem desperate. Courage is not, as some people think, the absence of fear. Everyone feels afraid at some point; we're all human. Some think of Marines as superhuman beings who do not feel normal emotions. In fact, they simply have the determination to go onward a little further.

Bomb Disposal in the Military

Explosive Ordnance Disposal (EOD) teams are extensively trained to diffuse different types of bombs and explosives in any environment. EOD technicians might be asked to parachute out of an airplane, deploy from a helicopter, or dive underwater to take care of torpedoes or other explosives. EOD technicians need to know in-depth information about many different types of explosives, including nuclear weapons, as well as information about decontamination procedures.

Being an EOD technician is an extremely high-stress job. Loving the adrenaline or having nerves of steel are a necessary requirement!

The Marines look for people who show courage in their daily lives, such as standing up for what they feel is right even when everybody else might be against them. Courage is vital, because if soldiers do not do their duty in combat, other people's lives may be lost. For those Marines who are trained to parachute into dangerous situations, it takes courage to make that leap out of the plane—but it takes still more courage to follow through with a mission, no matter how dangerous. It's that quality—the determination to keep going and do your best, even when you're afraid—that means you have what it takes to be a Marine.

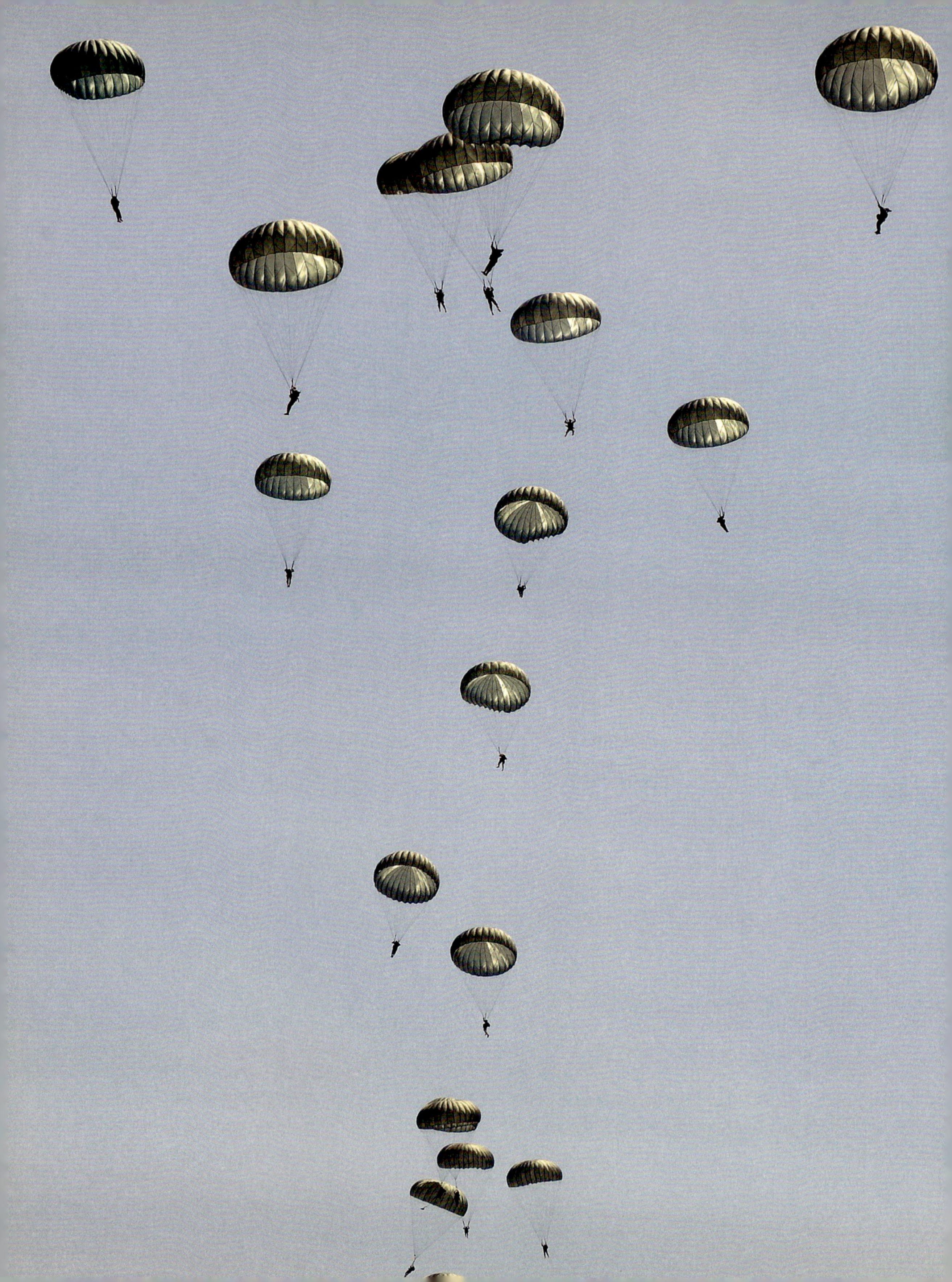

CHAPTER 7
Paratrooper Missions Around the World

Paratroopers in the Army, the Air Force, and the Marines have served their nation well in the past—and today they continue to work hard for their country. In the twenty-first century, their skill, dedication, and courage are making a difference all around the world.

HUMANITARIAN AID

Paratroopers will not only serve their country in combat. The U.S. military may call on them to help other countries that are in need.

HAITIAN EARTHQUAKE

On January 12, 2010, the island country of Haiti suffered from a strong earthquake. It was the sixth-deadliest earthquake ever recorded, and up to 300,000 Haitians died.

One million victims of the earthquake became homeless; this is comparable to the entire population of Montana not knowing where they will sleep the next day. Two days after the hurricane struck, paratroopers from the Eighty-Second Airborne Division were in Port-Au-Prince, the capital of Haiti, amid crumbling buildings under a scorching Caribbean sun. The Eighty-Second Airborne Division distributed food, handed out water, and provided medical care. By the end of January, the paratroopers began a "food surge," in which they handed out one million pounds of food each day. This allowed for Haitians to focus energy on rebuild-

Tommy Clark of Team D, First Battalion, 325th Airborne Infantry Regiment, Second Brigade Combat Team, 82nd Airborne Division, hands bottled water to a local Haitian woman. This was the second food drop in Haiti for "Red Falcons."

ing rather than searching for food. The paratroopers also employed Haitians to be guides, drivers, and interpreters. They interviewed thousands for these positions. While they were interviewed, they received key information on areas that were in need of assistance. The Airborne troops provided a needed service for the Haitians: clearing out rubble. They worked with a local construction company to clean up the streets of Port-Au-Prince. Clean streets meant easier access for food and medicine to those in need.

The paratroopers are using their resources to help others. Captain Jason Alexander of the Airborne Field Artillery Regiment stated, "These are guys here who just hit the ground and they're already helping," while a cannon crewmember with the Airborne Field Artillery Regiment stated, "We're doing good here . . . we're doing the best job we can." These teams give everything they have, every day, regardless of whether the mission involves giving enemy forces gunfire or giving earthquake victims food.

A BIG BOOST: HUMANITARIAN MISSION IN THE PHILIPPINES

The Philippine government and United States have been allies for a long time. The U.S. military trained Philippine troops in the past, but in 2009, the Philippines needed a different form of help from the Navy SEALs. After Typhoon Ketsana flooded the Philippine Islands, the United States provided assistance to our ally. Many were affected by the flooding that swept through the nation, and the typhoon hit Manila especially hard. Hundreds of thousands of people lost their homes.

A paratrooper with Third Platoon, Company D, First Battalion, 504th Parachute Infantry Regiment, First Brigade, 82nd Airborne Division, hands out snacks to local children while conducting border interdiction operations along the Iraqi-Syrian border in Iraq. The platoon of paratroopers redistributed care packages intended for themselves to poor farmers.

Navy SEALs provided support to towns affected. They engaged in rescue operations for residents of towns and villages devastated by the typhoon. The SEALs transported displaced Filipinos to churches and schools. Teams also delivered food and fresh water where it was needed. Their ability to parachute into hard-to-reach areas gave these teams added flexibility.

A Filipino congressman stated, "The work the U.S. Military did was terrific. . . . I was very thankful for U.S. support. Your teams were able to successfully go to Santa Lucia High School to help deliver food. It was a big boost that your people were helping us out."

PARATROOPERS IN ACTION

INVADING IRAQ

In March 2003, the 173rd Airborne Brigade was there for a moment in history, the invasion of Iraq. One thousand paratroopers deployed into Kurdish-controlled Northern Iraq, a location that is more friendly to U.S. troops than the rest of the country.

For some of the paratroopers, it was their first jump since leaving training. Others had more experience, but for all parties involved, it was a tense moment. Private Jerry Allen recalls, "I had never seen so many planes in my life."

Just like many other military operations, not everything went perfectly by plan. A storm had passed over the previous day, and because of this, many troopers fell deep into the mud. Walking through the muddy terrain used up time and energy for the soldiers.

Once the paratroopers got out of the mud, they fought off Saddam Hussein's forces and seized an airfield. The airfield was a strategic boost to the beginning of the Iraq war. Later, Kurds assisted the U.S. army in fighting off **insurgents**. Well-trained troops using the element of surprise through the use of parachutes proved an effective strategy during the invasion of Iraq.

PARATROOPERS IN AFGHANISTAN

The "rendezvous with destiny" William Lee spoke of when he founded the paratroopers has been met. Today, the 101st Division is making history. By the end of 2010, nearly 20,000 troops in Afghanistan deployed by parachute to defeat the Taliban, surprising them at every step.

The Navy SEALs also used parachuting equipment for both the invasion of Afghanistan and Iraq. These specialized units infiltrated enemy land to gain the element of surprise and deploy with speed. Parachute technology is integral to inserting specialized teams for information collecting and performing specialized missions.

THE INVASION OF MARJA

When the United States routed out the Taliban from Marjah in Afghanistan, they sent in Marine soldiers to support combat operations. Parts of the area were still controlled by

UNDERSTAND THE FULL MEANING

insurgents: Rebels.

Private First Class Matthew Fram, a chemical specialist with Battery B, Third Battalion, 319th Field Artillery Regiment, First Brigade, 82nd Airborne Division, waits at the airfield to load an aircraft at Al Asad Air Base. Fram is deployed to Iraq in support of Operation Iraqi Freedom.

the Taliban, and the Marines were part of President Barack Obama's push to add more troops into Afghanistan.

Operation Moshtarak was one of the largest military operations since the initial invasion of Afghanistan. The mission was to take over much of the land dominated by the Taliban and drug dealers. The production and sale of poppy plants in Afghanistan is one of the biggest elements of the local economy. Poppies make opium and heroin, which is the main source of life for 60 to 70 percent of farmers in the south of Afghanistan. Money from poppy sales also makes billions of dollars for **extremists** in Afghanistan.

All Marines are trained to deploy out of a helicopter. Their success in the operation at Marjah involved jumping from the Osprey, a special military aircraft that looks like a combination of a helicopter and small airplane.

A Marine invading Marja would deal with the constant threat of IEDs (roadside bombs) as they entered. These bombs are common, but Marine forces reported a larger than usual network of booby traps and bombs as they entered the city. To get through the traps, the marines navigated through with special mine-clearing vehicles.

The gunfire the troops saw on the battleground in Marja was scary enough, but even worse were Afghani snipers who hid from sight. Joshua T. Hurst, a Marine who participated in the invasion of Marja, spoke about the experience of entering the warzone: "We started taking small-arms and indirect fire from every direction. Rounds were cracking over

UNDERSTAND THE FULL MEANING

extremists: People who hold extreme and often dangerous views.

> ### "FORMER" PARATROOPER
> After you have completed your duty for the United States, you will never be called an "ex-paratrooper" or a "former paratrooper." Once a paratrooper, always a paratrooper.

our heads. . . . When the snipers started to shoot, my frustrations reached their peak. [I was] thinking, 'if I move an inch I'm going to get shot.'" Once the bombs had been cleared and the first wave of shooting was done, the Marines quickly tried to maintain power in the area. But tensions were high.

James R. Borzillieri, a gunner who participated in the operation, spoke to a reporter about the need to be adaptable. "The only thing that really prepped me for this deployment was my last. Nothing you can do to prepare, except do it. . . . Trying to prepare for combat, you need to understand that you can't control who gets hit or who's coming back. You just have to keep your head down and fire back. Keeping your composure is key."

But the Marines succeeded. They took over Marja from the Taliban, a major victory in the war after a series of setbacks. General Charles Hudson stated that Operation Moshtarak was an event "that will go down in Marine Corps history."

"Swift, Silent, Deadly."
—motto of the Marines Reconnaissance Team

Members of the U.S. Navy parachute demonstration team, the Leap Frogs, perform a tri-plane formation during a rehearsal for the Ocean City Air Show. The Leap Frogs are based in San Diego and perform parachute demonstrations across the United States supporting Naval Special Warfare and the Navy Recruiting Command.

PERFORMING DOMESTICALLY

One of the most fun and danger-free missions a Navy Paratrooper performs is at an air-show. There they perform stunts for crowds of people across the country.

At Army-Navy games, paratroopers often land on the football field during a down-time in the game. Paratroopers also do synchronized jumping, jumping with jetpacks and other feats of jumping skill to adoring crowds.

HEROES IN THE SKY

During World War II, a woman named Anne Archer Tullidge, the mother of a paratrooper, put together a collection of quotes and Bible verses for her son. She sent it to him to encourage him as he jumped again and again into danger. When he died at D-Day, his parents made copies of the little book and distributed it to other paratroopers.

One of the quotes in the book is by a man named Josh Billings: "Heroism is simple, and yet it is rare. Everyone who does the best he can is a hero."

That is the challenge we see in the lives of paratroopers, both those who fought in earlier wars and those who are fulfilling their duties today. We do not all have the opportunity to leap from a plane and fall through the sky, down to the land where a dangerous and important mission awaits us. But we can all do our best.

FIND OUT MORE ON THE INTERNET

Air Force www.airforce.com

Army Recruiting www.goarmy.com

Department of Defense www.defense.gov

Marine Corps www.marines.com

Navy www.navy.com

U.S. Naval Academy www.usna.edu

West Point www.usma.edu

The websites listed on this page were active at the time of publication. The publisher is not responsible for websites that have changed their address or discontinued operation since the date of publication. The publisher will review and update the websites upon each reprint.

FURTHER READING

Bryant, Russ and Susan. *Screaming Eagles: 101st Airborne Division.* St. Paul, Minn.: Zenith Press, 2007.

Hirsh, Michael. *None Braver: U.S. Air Force Pararescuemen in the War on Terrorism.* New York: NAL Caliber, 2003.

Mast, Gregory, and Hans Halberstadt. *To Be a Paratrooper.* St. Paul, Minn.: Zenith Press, 2007.

Pushies, Fred J. *82nd Airborne*. Minneapolis, Minn.: Zenith Press, 2008.

Sandler, Michael. *Pararescuemen in Action.* New York: Bearport Publishing, 2008.

BIBLIOGRAPHY

101st Airborne Division, en.wikipedia.org/wiki/101st_Airborne_Division (10 June 2010).

Army, "Operation Unified Response," www.army.mil/-news/2010/03/25/36388-operation-unified-response/ (10 June 2010).

Army, "Paratroopers prep for U.S-Iraqi combined Training," www.army.mil/-news/2010/02/17/34529-paratroopers-prep-for-us-iraqi-combined-training/ (10 June 2010).

Army, "Soldier Life, Airborne School," www.goarmy.com/life/airborne_school.jsp (10 June 2010).

Army, "Soldiers Test New Parachute," armylive.dodlive.mil/index.php/2009/09/soldiers-test-new-parachute/ (10 June 2010).

Atkinson, Rick, "The Single Most Effective Weapon Against our Deployed Forces," *Washington Post*, www.washingtonpost.com/wp-dyn/content/story/2007/09/29/ST2007092900754.html?sid=ST2007092900754 (10 June 2010).

Dilanian, Ken, "Airborne Jumps into Northern Iraq," *Free Republic*, www.freerepublic.com/focus/f-news/876654/posts (10 June 2010).

Manny, Gamallo, "Oklahoma soldier killed in Afghanistan," *Tulsa World*, www.tulsaworld.com/news/article.aspx?subjectid=12&articleid=20100305_12_0_hrimgs648776 (10 June 2010).

Navy, "Explosive Ordnance Disposal Technician," www.navy.com/navy/careers/special-operations/eod.html (10 June 2010).

Navy, "EOD Divers Train with Kenyans," www.navy.mil/search/display.asp?story_id=19133 (10 June 2010).

Navy, "Expeditionary Sailors Defuse Mock IEDs, Prep for Upcoming Deployments," www.navy.mil/search/display.asp?story_id=24093 (10 June 2010).

Navy, "Navy Identifies SEAL who Died During Training Exercise," www.navy.mil/search/display.asp?story_id=35032 (10 June 2010).

Schulte, Adrian "Paratroopers remember the jump into Iraq," www.hqusareur.army.mil/htmlinks/Press_Releases/2004/Mar2004/23Mar2004-01.htm (10 June 2010).

INDEX

Advanced Airborne School 19
Air Force Pararescue 29, 30, 32, 35, 37–38, 40
Air Rescue Service (ARS) 13
air-show 89
American Eagles 44, 46
Army Parachute Team 43, 44, 46, 48–49
Army Physical Fitness Test (APFT) 49

barometric trigger 26
Black Hats 17
Blanchard 10
boot camp 59, 76–77

chemical warfare 35

Da Vinci, Leonardo 9, 12
Department of Defense 30
D-Day 89

espionage 65
Explosive Ordinance Disposal (EOD) 76

guerrilla 54

helicopters 40, 43, 74, 86
High-Altitude, High-Opening (HAHO) 27
High-Altitude, Low-Opening (HALO) 26–27
humanitarian aid 79, 81–83
Hussein, Saddam 84

jumpmaster 19–20, 38

Kennedy, John F. 54

Lenormand, Louis-Sebastien 10–11

Marine Paratroopers 65, 66, 68–75

Navy SEALs 53, 54, 56, 59–60, 63
Nazis 15, 43–44
Nicholas, Adrian 12

Obama, Barack 86
observation balloon 10

Paid Parachutist Positions (PPP) 19
parajumper (PJ) 13, 15, 30, 35, 37, 40
paratrooper 17–24, 26–27

Reagan, Ronald 54
reconnaissance 6, 44, 65–66, 69
Renaissance 10

static line drop 19, 26, 37

Taliban 44, 84, 86–87

U.S. Army Airborne School 17, 37

Vietti-Teppa, Olivier 12

wind tunneling 38
World War
    I 10–12, 66
    II 12, 15, 43–46, 89

PICTURE CREDITS

U.S. Air and Space: p. 11
U.S. Air Force: pp. 28, 31, 33, 34, 36, 39
U.S. Army: pp. 8, 16, 18, 21, 23, 25, 42, 45, 49, 51, 80, 82, 85
U.S. Department of Defense: pp. 64, 68, 71, 78
U.S. Navy: pp. 52, 55, 57, 58, 61, 62, 73, 88

To the best knowledge of the publisher, all images not specifically credited are in the public domain. If any image has been inadvertently uncredited, please notify Harding House Publishing Service, 220 Front Street, Vestal, New York 13850, so that credit can be given in future printings.

ABOUT THE AUTHOR

Jack Montana lives in upstate New York with his wife and three dogs. He writes on military survival, health, and wellness. He graduated from Binghamton University.

ABOUT THE CONSULTANT

Colonel John Carney, Jr. is USAF-Retired, President and the CEO of the Special Operations Warrior Foundation.

CC

Central Childrens